Billy Jones,
Dog Star

Siân Lewis

Illustrated by
Maggy Roberts

PONT READALONE

First Impression—2002

ISBN 1 84323 169 7

© text: Siân Lewis, 2003

© illustrations: Maggy Roberts, 2003

For Stu – M.R.

This volume is published with the financial support of the
Welsh Books Council.

Printed in Wales at
Gomer Press, Llandysul, Ceredigion SA44 4QL

For Rhodri

Chapter 1

When this story begins, Billy Jones wasn't famous. He was just an ordinary dog living with his family in No. 7 Panteg Road. Billy lived with Mam and Dad Jones and their children, Catrin aged eleven, Tom aged ten, and Emma, who was nearly seven and a half.

The Jones family weren't exactly an ordinary family.

Dad Jones was good at singing.

Mam Jones was good at playing the piano.

Catrin and Tom were good at singing, reciting AND playing the piano.

Emma was good at singing too, though she'd given up at the age of seven and a quarter, when the family had first moved into No. 7 Panteg Road.

The only one who had never been on stage was Billy Jones, but then, of course, he was a dog.

One Saturday morning in September the Jones family had all got up early. In the bathroom Dad was gargling because he had a tickly throat. In the front room Mam was playing the piano for Catrin and Tom. In her bedroom Emma was drawing a picture on a piece of pink card and Billy was standing on his hind legs looking out of the window.

Billy was watching the blue tits peck at the peanut feeder in Mrs Batley's garden next door. They all flew away when Sam, the builder, walked up the garden path. Billy jumped away smartly too, in case Mrs Batley came out and blamed him for frightening the birds. Mrs Batley didn't like barking dogs. She didn't like noise of any kind. That's why Emma had stopped singing since she came to Panteg Road.

Billy went to push his nose under Emma's arm. Emma had just finished her picture. She'd drawn a small brown and white blob. Underneath was a larger brown and white blob with four black lines hanging down and another sticking out at the back.

'That's a picture of you, Billy,' she said, holding it up.

Billy wagged his tail. He knew what was coming next, because he often helped Emma write letters to her friends. First Emma pulled out the secret stamp from under her bed. The secret

stamp was a thing that looked like a black and slimy mushroom, but was actually a piece of blue bath sponge, that Emma had rolled in mud. As soon as the secret stamp was placed in front of him, Billy put his right paw on it. Next he pressed his muddy paw on the back of the pink card, beneath a message that said 'From Billy and Emma' with lots of Xs.

'Good dog, Billy,' said Emma and she sat with her arm round him, while she blew on the pawprint to dry it.

In the bathroom Dad had finished gargling. He poked his head round the door and mouthed, 'Okay, Em?'

'Yes,' said Emma, hiding the card behind her back.

'Good,' mouthed Dad. He couldn't speak because he was saving his voice. He and Catrin and Tom were going to sing at an eisteddfod that afternoon. So he raised his thumb and off he went downstairs. He took the newspaper out of the letterbox and settled down to read it in the kitchen.

As soon as he'd gone, Emma fetched a crumpled brown envelope from the drawer of her desk and slipped the pink card inside. On the envelope she wrote "Mrs Batley". Then she put her hand on Billy's head and whispered, 'Stay, Billy! Good dog. Stay!'

Billy did as he was told. He sat still and listened to Emma's soft footsteps on the stairs and the creak of the front door. But when he heard her creep along the garden path, he just had to jump up and run across to the window to make sure she was safe.

When Billy saw Emma's curly head beneath him, the hairs stood up on the back of his neck. She was creeping across the lawn towards the fence that separated No. 7 Panteg Road from No. 8. She didn't realise that the fierce Mrs Batley was on the other side of that fence with Sam the builder. What if Mrs Batley shouted at her? Emma hated being shouted at. Billy barked a warning. He barked so loudly that Tom came running up the stairs.

'Hey, Billy,' called Tom, as he burst into the bedroom. 'Come downstairs. We've got news for you.'

Billy tried to dive past him. He wanted to get out to save Emma, but Tom picked him up in his arms and bundled him down the stairs.

In the kitchen Dad was reading the paper, Mam was leaning over his shoulder and Catrin was dancing around. They all turned and beamed at the little brown and white terrier.

'Billy!' said Catrin. 'You're going to go on stage.' She ran over and hugged him.

'On stage?' said a small voice.

Emma had come rushing back in. Billy wriggled out of Tom's arms, ran to her and jumped up. Emma put her arms round him.

'Why is Billy going on stage?' she asked.

'Ah!' said Mam. To save Dad's voice, she took the paper from him, coughed importantly and read out loud: 'Dog actor wanted for Christmas pantomime.'

'Dog actor!' said Emma.

'That'll be our Billy,' said Mam with a smile.

Chapter 2

Billy barked. He knew that that particular Saturday was an eisteddfod day in No. 7 Panteg Road.

This is what usually happened on eisteddfod days.

First the Jones family had an early breakfast.

Then they practised their songs, all except Emma.

They had a bath and washed their hair.

They ate a small, healthy lunch.

They put on clean clothes.

Lastly they all drove off in the car to the eisteddfod, leaving Billy, their brown and white terrier, home alone.

Billy didn't like eisteddfod days. He didn't like being shut out of the front room while the others practised. He didn't like the strong smell of hair gel and bath oil. He didn't like not being allowed to jump up on the children, in case he dirtied their clothes. And he certainly didn't like feeling left out.

But this eisteddfod day was different.

First of all Mam read the advertisement again.

'Dog actor wanted for Christmas pantomime,' she read. 'Must be bright, affectionate and well-behaved. For more information phone Theatr Seirian.'

'Billy's bright, affectionate and well-behaved,' said Catrin, hopping around and beaming at Billy as Mam reached for the phone.

Everyone went quiet, while Mam talked to the man on the other end of the line.

'Oh yes, Billy can do that,' she kept saying. 'Billy can do that.'

Billy barked excitedly at the sound of his name. He barked even more, when Mam put the phone down, turned round and bowed in front of him. She bowed so low that her red hair swept the ground.

'Your wish is my command, Lord Ruffles,' she said.

'Has Billy got the part in the pantomime already?' Tom gasped.

'Not yet,' said Mam tossing her hair back with a giggle, 'but he's got an audition next Saturday morning at ten o'clock. The pantomime is a special version of Cinderella and Billy's going to try for the part of Ruffles, the prince's dog.'

'What will he have to do in the audition?' asked Catrin.

'First of all he has to pretend he's sitting on a chair in the prince's ballroom,' explained Mam. 'He has to sit very, very quietly and not get excited. Then, for the scene when the prince takes the glass slipper to Cinderella's house, he has to catch hold of Cinderella's apron and pull her onto the stage.'

'Easy! Easy!' said Tom, drumming his fists on the table. 'I bet Billy wins.'

'And then he'll be a performer just like us,' said Catrin.

'Ruff!' said Billy.

'Ruff-les,' said Mam and everyone laughed, everyone except Emma who had gone back upstairs.

Mam even got a Doggie Treat out of the cupboard and gave it to Billy for no reason at all.

Then Catrin said, 'Can Bill . . . Ruffles, I mean, sit in the front room and listen to us singing? He'll have to sit quietly and that'll be good practice for him.'

'Good idea,' mouthed Dad. He jumped up, looked at Mam, pointed his finger at the ceiling and, when she nodded, he clicked his fingers at

Tom and Catrin and the three of them ran up to Mam and Dad's bedroom.

Billy went to hide under the table, when things started thumping and bumping above his head. He growled in dismay when a strange-looking creature came clumping down the stairs. But it was only Dad, bent double, with Mam's best bedroom chair on his back and Tom and Catrin hanging on to its golden legs. The chair had slender, curved arms and a blue velvet seat and back. Dad had bought it in an antique shop and mended it especially for Mam. It looked a very fine chair, just exactly the sort of chair that you might find in a prince's ballroom.

Dad and Tom and Catrin carried the chair into the front room, then they all turned round and looked at Billy. Catrin patted the chair seat and Tom made that strange noise again, that sounded like a bark.

'Ruffles! Ruffles!' he called.

Billy barked back rather snappily. Dad, Tom and Catrin were being very silly, he thought. They knew he wasn't allowed to sit on any chair and he certainly wasn't allowed to sit on that one. He'd tried it often when he was a pup, but Mam and Dad had said 'Down, Billy!' in such stern voices that he'd soon given up. Anyway it was time he went upstairs to play with Emma, so he came out from under the table, shook himself and off he went with a leap and a bound.

Billy had almost got as far as the landing, when he heard a rattle-rattle-rattle behind him. It was Mam. She was standing at the foot of the stairs with the packet of Doggie Treats in her hand.

'Ruffles! Ruffles!' she called.

Billy turned right round.

'Ruffles! Ruffles!' called Mam and she disappeared through the front room door.

Billy crept down and peeped through the banister. To his surprise Mam took out a Doggie Treat and put it on the seat of the golden chair. At once he took a flying leap, skidded across the hallway, ran into the front room and slid his nose onto the blue velvet seat. He had just got his teeth round the Doggie Treat, when Mam pushed him up onto the chair and held him there. Billy was so astonished he swallowed the Treat whole. And what did everyone do? Did they shout "Down Billy!"? No, they didn't. They clapped him – all except Emma, of course, because she wasn't there.

'Good dog!' said Catrin, hugging him.

'He looks just like a prince's dog,' said Tom.

'Emma!' called Mam. 'Come and see Ruffles sitting on the golden chair.'

After a while there was a squeaking noise as Emma slid her hand slowly down the banister. She stopped on the last step but one and stared with her thumb in her mouth.

'That's not Ruffles,' she said. 'That's Billy.'

Then she turned round and went back upstairs.

After she'd gone, Tom whispered in Billy's ear, 'Emma's scared of performing because Mrs Batley shouted at us. But you don't have to be scared.'

'No, of course not,' said Mam. 'A noble dog like you doesn't have to be afraid of anything.' She tickled Billy's ears and giggled.

Billy opened his mouth and grinned back at her.

He liked sitting on the golden chair. The blue padded seat was soft and comfortable. From the chair he could see the birds fluttering in Mrs Batley's garden. He could see Mrs Batley too. His sharp ears had heard her footsteps on the lawn. She was pulling out a brown envelope that Emma had pushed in between the slats of the fence.

Billy gave a small warning growl, but he soon shushed when Dad gave him a sharp look. What did he care about Mrs Batley anyway? He was an important dog who was attending a rehearsal. He pricked up his ears and sat proudly listening to Catrin and Tom. Then, when they'd finished singing, he carefully thumped his tail on the golden chair.

Chapter 3

As soon as he got up the next morning, Billy rushed in to check that the golden chair was still in the front room. It was, so he sat on it and listened to the blue tits twitter on the fence. The blue tits flew off into Mrs Batley's garden one after another and then came back again.

Billy's tail shivered slightly. When he and his family had come to live in No. 7 Panteg Road two and a half months before, he hadn't been used to birds. He hadn't been used to a big garden with trees and bushes either. The first time he was let out, Billy had gone racing down the path. When a cloud of birds flew up in the air in front of him, he thought it was a good game. So he barked as loud as he could and did it again.

That was when Mrs Batley had poked her head over the fence.

'I hope you're going to keep that dog under control,' she'd said to Mam.

'Oh yes,' said Mam, whose face had gone bright red. 'I'm sorry. He's just a bit overexcited.'

Billy had got overexcited again that very afternoon. Emma was tossing a ball in the air and Billy wanted to show her that he could toss a whole lot of birds into the air without even touching them. He'd just given one loud bark and sent a couple of finches diving for cover, when Mrs Batley shouted over the fence 'Stop that!' Then she'd said in a loud voice, 'Really! People mustn't be allowed to keep dogs, if they can't discipline them.'

Emma had cowered behind the lilac bush. Her eyes were big and scared-looking. No one had ever shouted at her and Billy before. When Mrs Batley had gone back into the house, she had squeezed Billy hard and whispered in his ear, 'You've got to stop scaring the birds, or she'll send you away. If you stop barking, I'll stop singing. Promise?'

Billy had licked her face, which was as good as a promise. Then Emma had spat on the back of her hand and stamped Billy's paw on it. That was their Top Secret sign.

Since that day Billy hadn't chased the birds. Mam and Dad had warned him not to and, anyway, he'd got bored with them. They were just silly feathered things that couldn't sit still to eat. They flitted back and forth, back and forth, to the bird table all day long, instead of having one good meal from a bowl.

So after a while Billy yawned, jumped down from his golden chair and tip-tapped very quietly into the hallway, so as not to wake anyone up. He'd invented another game, called "Hunt the Prizes", which he always played after every eisteddfod day.

The day before the Jones family had gone to

the eisteddfod without him as usual, and late at night they'd brought home a collection of prizes. They'd brought a large silver cup, a small silver cup and two small wooden shields with pictures of musical notes on the front.

Billy went round the house hunting for those prizes. First he sniffed out the large silver cup. It was sitting in Dad's special glass cupboard in the front room. Now he sniffed his way up the stairs and poked his nose round the door of Tom's room. He spotted the small silver cup straight away. It was standing on top of Tom's PlayStation right next to a wooden shield. Next he moved on to Catrin's neat and tidy room. Catrin kept all her shiny cups and shields on the shelves above her desk. All the shields looked the same to Billy, but he was sure the new one was there somewhere. It usually was.

Billy gave a satisfied whine. The whine meant "Game over". He'd won again. He always did. He went to see if Emma was awake, but she was fast asleep, so he lay down and waited on the mat beside her bed.

He was still waiting, when the door of Mam and Dad's room opened and out came Dad in a green dressing-gown.

'Hi there, Ruffles!' Dad said cheerily, when he saw Billy. He was speaking properly, though not very loud, so as not to disturb anyone.

Billy jumped up and ran out to him. He remembered the magic word "Ruffles!" from the day before and he knew it meant fun.

'Hi there, Ruffles,' said Dad again. He jiggled the belt of his dressing-gown above Billy's head.

Billy jumped and caught it in his teeth. Dad tried to pull it back and they had a tug-of-war, which Billy won. He pulled Dad right across the landing.

'Good dog!' said Dad, then he clamped his hand over his mouth, because he'd shouted out loud without meaning to.

In all four bedrooms in No. 7 Panteg Road, there were squeaks and grunts, as everyone woke up and tried to work out what was happening. Dad dived quickly into the bathroom and came out again with a shower cap on his head.

Tom and Catrin tumbled out onto the landing, followed by Mam. Emma peeped round the door of her room.

'What are you doing, Dad?' cried Catrin.

'Oh!' said Dad in a squeaky voice. 'I'm Cinderella and I've just been pulled out of the kitchen by Ruffles the dog. Watch this!' He dangled the belt above Billy's head again and Billy caught it and pulled.

Mam gasped, but she didn't say, 'Stop it, Billy!' as she normally would. In fact she giggled, even though Billy had left tooth marks on the belt. 'You're not Cinderella,' she said to Dad. 'You're her Ugly Sister. Isn't that right, Em?'

'Em can play Cinderella,' said Dad. 'Come on, Em!'

'She can be Cinderemma!' said Tom. He rushed back into his room and snatched the first

thing he saw, which was the small silver cup. 'This is a pretend glass slipper. Take it to her Ruffles! Take it to Cinderemma!'

Billy didn't, because Emma had already closed the door of her room. But he did sit down with the silver cup between his paws. He looked so proud that Tom rushed to take a photo of him, before taking the cup away and putting it back on his desk.

Chapter 4

'If Billy wins the audition, we'll have to get him his own silver cup,' said Catrin.

'Yeah!' said Tom.

Mam, Dad, Catrin and Tom were having their breakfast.

As soon as they'd finished, Tom said, 'Let's all act Cinderella now, so Ruffles can have a proper dress rehearsal.'

'Yes!' said Mam. 'And we must try and get Emma to join in.'

So everyone ran back upstairs and started rooting around in their cupboards just like dogs digging for bones. Billy stood on the landing and wagged his tail, as people rushed past with their arms full of clothes and sparkly things. Even Emma came out to watch. Mam persuaded her to put on a blue bridesmaid dress that Catrin had worn when she was six years old and helped her tie some tinsel round her hair.

'There we are,' said Mam. 'Now you're Cinderemma. Isn't she beautiful, Ruffles?'

Billy barked.

Mam herself wasn't looking too good. Her cheeks were like red balloons with black spots painted on them and she was wearing Tom's rugby socks and Dad's most massive green T-shirt. When she opened her mouth, her teeth fell out. Billy backed away and growled.

'You're a brilliant Ugly Sister, Mam,' said Tom with a giggle. 'You've scared Billy.'

'Ruff!' said Billy in alarm.

Something even worse had stepped out of Mam and Dad's bedroom. It was a thing with green hair and eyes that popped out. It had big hairy arms and a flowery dress that didn't fit. Billy rushed to the safety of Emma's bedroom, but even Emma was laughing.

'That's Dad,' she said. 'He's wearing Catrin's Halloween wig and silly glasses. He's an Ugly Sister too, Billy.'

Billy peeped round Emma's legs. Thank goodness Tom and Catrin were still looking fairly normal. Catrin was wearing Mam's long silk nightie with a silver band in her hair and she carried a silver wand in her hand. Tom was wearing black jeans and a black shirt with a red bow tie. He was the prince, of course. His hair was shiny and stuck up at the front, but his voice, when he spoke, was very posh and strange.

'Come, my good dog Ruffles,' he said. 'Let us go to the ball.'

He picked Billy up and carried him downstairs with the others following.

Billy was put to sit on the golden chair in the front room and Mam said to him in her normal voice, 'This is the prince's ballroom. You be a good dog and practise sitting very quietly, while we dance around you.' Then she pulled a Doggie Treat from her left rugby sock and gave it to him.

Billy tossed it in the air, swallowed it and settled down to watch with an astonished smile on his face. He'd never seen anything quite like it in all his time with the Jones family. First everyone except Catrin went out into the hallway. Catrin herself sat at the piano, waved her wand in the air and said in a loud voice, 'Let the ball begin.'

As soon as Catrin started playing a tinkly dance tune, in walked Tom with Emma on his arm. They danced round and round very nicely till Mam and Dad barged through the door. Billy gaped in dismay. Mam and Dad were absolutely useless at dancing. They were like galloping horses. They knocked into things. They pushed into Tom and Emma. They even talked in silly voices.

'Oh, pwince,' said Dad. 'Come and dance with lovely little me.'

'No, ickle me!' said Mam and she gave Dad a shove.

Billy stood up on the chair. He was all for barking at Mam and Dad, when Catrin slowly began to thump out a row of single notes, that sounded like a clock striking.

'Oh,' said Emma. 'It's midnight. It's time for me to go.' She left Tom and ran out of the room, leaving one of her pink sandals behind.

'Stop, Ruffles,' called Mam in a normal voice before he could run out after her.

Billy wasn't sure that he should listen to Mam after such a performance, but Mam collapsed onto the chair beside him and gave him a Doggie Treat.

'Oh, you are a good dog,' she said. 'If you can sit still through all that noise, you'll be able to get through the audition easily.'

'Ea-sy! Ea-sy!' said Tom.

Mam gave Billy another Doggie Treat and stroked his head while he ate it.

'Emma has gone to change into an old dress and an apron,' she explained. 'When she's ready, you can practise pulling her into the room, so the prince can put the sandal on her foot. She won't be a minute.'

Just then the back door clicked open and Mam looked round.

'Emma?' she called in a sharp voice. 'Emma!'

No one answered.

Mam got up and Billy tumbled off the chair. He ran after Mam into the kitchen. Emma's dance dress was on the floor, but there was no sign of Emma herself. Billy ran to the back door, clawed it wide open and rushed out onto the patio.

What he saw made him bark in dismay. Emma was standing at the fence talking to Mrs Batley. When her anxious little face turned towards him, Billy ran to the rescue. A cloud of birds rose from the bushes as he raced across the lawn.

'Ruffles! Ruffles!' shrieked Mam and Dad and Tom and Catrin.

'Ruffles!' snapped Mrs Batley as Billy got hold of Emma's apron and started pulling her away. 'You haven't got another dog surely? I thought your dog was called Billy.'

'He is,' said Emma in a squeaky voice, 'but he's acting in a pantomime.'

'Pantomime!' said Mrs Batley, glaring at the

strange painted figure of Mam who was running across the garden in Tom's rugby socks. 'I'd say it was always a pantomime in your house.'

Then she turned on her heel and walked away.

Emma wouldn't act after that. Mam blamed Mrs Batley for frightening her.

'Why did you have to go out in the garden anyway?' asked Mam, when they were all safely back in the house.

'Because Mrs Batley waved to me,' said Emma. 'She wanted to say thank you for the card.'

'You sent a card to her?' gasped Catrin.

Emma nodded. She climbed on Dad's knee and buried her face in his neck.

'I sent a card from me and Billy,' she said in a muffled voice. 'I said we were sorry for scaring her birds and we wouldn't do it again. But then we did!'

'It wasn't Ruffles' fault,' said Tom, kneeling down to stroke Billy who was sitting rather anxiously at Dad's feet.

Billy barked at once and wagged his tail.

Of course it wasn't Ruffles' fault.

Ruffles could do what he liked. He was allowed to sit on chairs and have silver cups, just like everyone else in the Jones family.

It was brilliant being Ruffles.

Chapter 5

By the time Saturday came, Billy had almost forgotten what it was like to be plain old Billy Jones. He'd been Ruffles for one whole week.

For one whole week he'd been an important member of the Jones family and Saturday morning was the best time of all.

Saturday was the day of the audition.

The Jones family got up at eight o'clock in the morning. It was exactly like an eisteddfod day, except that Billy was the centre of attention.

The Jones family didn't do any practising. They helped Billy to practise instead.

The Jones family didn't have time for a bath. Instead they bathed Billy, blow-dried him and brushed him! By the time half past nine came Billy was the smartest, sweetest-smelling dog in town.

And when Mam got the car out of the garage, it was Billy who got in the back with Tom and Catrin, leaving Emma and Dad at home.

'Good luck in the audition!' Dad called to him. 'If you don't get the part, I'll eat my wig.' He stood on the doorstep and waved the Halloween wig in the air, as the car moved away.

Emma said nothing, but she too waved from the front room, though Billy didn't notice. He was practising sitting very still and at the same time looking out of the window to see where they were going.

First of all Mam drove down a road that Billy knew. They passed the park and Emma, Tom and

Catrin's school. Billy saw some children playing on the swings, but he didn't bark or jump up at the window. He just smiled at them. Then Mam turned down a quiet road lined with trees and drove towards a large old building that looked like a palace.

'That's the theatre!' said Tom with an excited grin. 'Catrin and Dad and I have been singing there.'

Mam parked at the side of the theatre next to a white car. A tall man with silvery hair had just got out of the car. He was opening the back door.

'Come on, Ruffles!' the man said.

Billy turned round in surprise.

'Not you,' whispered Catrin in his ear. 'That's another Ruffles.'

Another Ruffles! Billy couldn't believe it. A tiny Yorkshire terrier had leapt out of the back seat of the car. She landed neatly in her master's arms. Her coat was silky and shiny and her hair tied up in a red bow. The man and the dog went towards a door marked AUDITION at the side of the building. Billy jumped out of the car and he and the Jones family followed.

Inside the building was a maze of cool, quiet corridors. The man and the Yorkshire terrier had already disappeared, but the Joneses followed the arrow signs on the walls till they came to a swinging blue door. Mam opened it a little way and peeped in.

Billy peeped in too. He saw a big room with a row of chairs. On each chair sat a person or a dog. The Yorkshire terrier and her master sat at the end of the row. Next to them sat a Labrador, then a dachshund, a corgi and a little black barrel-shaped thing with a white face. They all turned round to look at Billy.

'Shhhh! Steady, Ruffles,' whispered the owner of the Labrador to her dog.

Billy's ears pricked up. So did the ears of the other four dogs in the room.

And then Billy understood! All these dogs wanted to be Ruffles. It wasn't just him. His tail wagged very slowly and he began to feel a little bit worried.

At the front of the room, sideways on, was a plush red chair on a low stage. Facing it, at a table, sat two women and a man. The woman in the middle smiled at the Jones family.

'Come and take a seat,' she called. 'It's Billy Jones, isn't it? We're about to begin.'

'Come on, Billy,' whispered Mam.

Billy followed Mam towards the row of chairs. All the dogs were sitting quietly apart from the Yorkshire terrier. She was sitting up and begging very prettily. As Billy walked past, she dived into her master's pocket, took out a tiny glass slipper, leapt down lightly and placed it on her master's foot.

'Show-off!' whispered Catrin to Tom.

As soon as the Jones family had settled, the smiling lady got up.

'Thank you all for coming to the audition for the Christmas pantomime,' she said. 'Now we don't want to keep you waiting any longer than is necessary, so we'll start straight away. The first to perform will be Tina Timpkins. Could we have Tina on the stage please?'

Billy's ears twitched. The Yorkshire terrier's owner had got to his feet. At a click of his fingers the little dog got up and trotted beside him with her long coat rippling like a ball-gown. She was so small she had to jump twice her height to get onto the stage and, once there, she had to be lifted onto the red chair.

She sat on the chair as still as a china ornament, but as soon as the cheerful judge put on an apron, Tina Timpkins launched herself through the air.

She leapt clean off the chair, caught the apron strings between her tiny teeth and hung there like a furry bobble.

Everyone smiled and clapped and clapped. Tina Timpkins was brilliant! But she wouldn't get the part, of course. Tina Timpkins was far too small. A little dog like that couldn't possibly act in a Christmas pantomime. It was too dangerous for her. She'd get squashed by the other actors' feet, no doubt about it.

Tom nudged Billy and gave him a thumbs-up. Billy did nothing. He was feeling very nervous in case it was his turn next.

He needn't have worried.

'And now it's the turn of Silas,' said the smiling lady.

Silas the dachshund was busy watching a fly crawl up his mistress's leg. When his name was called, he was taken by surprise. He jumped up in excitement and ran straight over the Labrador's tail. Megan the Labrador didn't like that at all. She snapped so nastily at Silas, that the dachshund dived straight under the stage instead of on top of it. That was the end of both Silas and Megan, because, although they both acted very well, everyone knew you couldn't have an excitable dog or a snappy dog in a Christmas pantomime.

Tom patted Billy whose mouth was open in astonishment. 'Three down, three to go,' he whispered in his ear.

It was the little barrel-shaped creature's turn next. His name was Humphrey. He had small eyes, small ears and a rather sad, plain face. His owner was a jolly-looking young man with lots of bushy brown hair.

'Come on, Humph!' he said.

At once Humphrey ambled over to the stage. He jumped up on the chair and sat facing the judges with such a dreamy look on his face that Billy thought he'd gone to sleep with his eyes open. When a van in the carpark backfired with a loud bang, the judge on the end dropped his glasses, but Humphrey didn't even blink or turn a hair. He wasn't asleep, though. He got down from the chair as soon as he was told and, when the smiling judge put on the apron, he got hold of the hem and pulled her slowly and quietly across the stage.

Catrin nudged Tom and pulled a face. 'He was good,' she said.

'No,' said Tom. 'He was too serious. They wanted a bright dog, remember?'

'Oh, yes!' said Catrin, cheering up.

The corgi called Tanwen came next. She was certainly bright. In fact she was too bright. When the judge put on the apron, Tanwen didn't just tug at the strings. She pulled the apron clean off and raced away with it. Everyone giggled, even Tanwen's owner.

And then at last it was Billy's turn.

Chapter 6

The smiling judge turned to face the audience.

'And now last, but not least, we have Billy Jones,' she said.

'Ea-sy! Ea-sy!' whispered Tom in Billy's ear.

'Good luck!' whispered Catrin.

They were both sitting with their fingers crossed, Billy noticed.

Billy got up and walked with Mam to the stage. It was strange, but now that it was his turn to perform he didn't feel nervous at all. In fact, he was looking forward to it so much that his tail wagged. He knew he could perform as well as those other dogs. He just knew it.

At a signal from Mam he jumped first onto the stage, then onto the red chair. There he sat as quietly as Humphrey, but with his head to one side and a big, eager smile on his face. His bright eyes watched the judges. In the audience Catrin and Tom nudged each other excitedly. Billy heard them, so he knew he was doing well.

'Thank you, Billy,' said the smiling judge. 'Now then . . .' She got to her feet and put on the apron.

Billy watched Mam. When Mam nodded, he leapt lightly off the chair. When Mam nodded again, Billy practically danced across the stage. He caught hold of the apron AND wagged his tail at the same time!

When the judge pretended to look surprised, Billy let go and barked, just as if he were talking to her. Then he caught hold of the apron again and pulled her right across the stage to the red chair.

It was perfect.

As soon as Billy stopped, absolutely everyone in the room began to clap. Even the dogs joined in with excited barks. And once again Billy's tail began to wag and wag and wag.

He'd done it!

There was no doubt about it. He'd won!

He was just like Tom and Catrin and all the talented members of the Jones family. He was a star.

Just then the swing doors at the end of the room opened and in came two young men pushing a trolley. On the trolley was a teapot, cups and saucers, a plateful of chocolate biscuits and a silvery sugar basin and milk jug.

'Tea's up!' called one of the young men.

'Yes, tea's up,' said the chief judge cheerfully. 'You all deserve it after working so hard. Help yourselves, everybody.'

And Billy did!

One minute he was standing on the stage wagging his tail while everyone clapped him. The next moment he was zipping down the room and helping himself to the sugar basin.

'Oh-oh!' said Mam to the judges, as Billy came running back, scattering sugar all over the place. 'He thinks it's a silver cup and he thinks he's won it.'

Billy was sure of it. He dropped the basin proudly at Mam's feet and would have rushed back for the silvery milk jug, if Mam hadn't stopped him. Mam's face was as red as her hair.

'No, Billy,' she said in a choky voice.

And that was when poor Billy realised that he hadn't really won a prize at all.

Chapter 7

The journey home was quiet and miserable. As soon as the car stopped, Dad and Emma came rushing out of the front door.

'Humphrey got the part,' said Tom, folding his arms and scowling at them. 'You wouldn't believe what a boring dog he was. Nice, but boring. Billy was tons better. Absolutely tons!'

'It was the judge's fault,' Catrin said angrily. 'If she hadn't said "Help yourselves", Billy wouldn't have gone for the sugar basin and he'd have won easily.' She explained what had happened to Dad and Emma.

Dad said nothing. He just chewed on the ends of his green wig, while Emma stroked Billy's sticky head.

'Ruff!' said Billy sadly.

No one replied with the magic word "Ruffles". In fact the word would never again be mentioned in No. 7 Panteg Road. And no one clapped Billy for trying to say it, though they petted him a lot and took him into the kitchen where Mam fed him a whole packet of Doggie Treats to try and cheer him up.

The Doggie Treats tasted like sawdust in Billy's mouth. While he was trying to eat them, he heard a bumpy noise on the stairs. He looked up just in time to see the legs of his golden chair disappear.

Billy was back to being an ordinary dog again. He plodded upstairs with Emma and sat very still on the bathroom floor, while she carefully sponged the sugar out of his fur.

'Don't look so sad, Billy,' said Emma, hugging him. 'You're still the best dog in the world.'

Billy knew that wasn't true. He followed her into the bedroom and sank down with his head on his paws and his eyes half-closed.

'You don't have to go on stage,' said Emma. 'There's other things you can do. You can come and help me make a card.'

But Billy didn't want to. He was no good at anything. He couldn't act in a pantomime. He couldn't draw pictures. All he could do was make a pawprint. So when Emma put her hand under the bed and brought out the secret stamp, Billy whined and pushed it away with his nose. When

Emma got her crayons out and started making a picture, he rolled over with his back to her. And when Emma finished her card and got to her feet, he pretended he was fast asleep.

Emma tiptoed out of the room and closed the door behind her.

Billy didn't care.

He went on pretending to be asleep, though sometimes his eyelids flickered. They flickered when the front door opened and closed. They flickered when his sharp ears picked up the sound of Emma's footsteps on the front path. And when he heard the click of the side gate, they opened wide.

Billy looked up suddenly. Shadows were swirling and swooping along the walls. He jumped up and ran across to the window. The air was full of birds and it was Emma who'd scared them! She was standing on Mrs Batley's front path with an envelope in her hands and Mrs Batley was coming round the corner of the house. Billy forgot all about being sad. He barked a warning.

When Emma didn't hear, he rushed to the door and clawed at it. From the direction of Mrs Batley's house came rumbles and snortings and creaks. Billy whined as loud as he could. He clawed and whined louder still, till Catrin ran upstairs and opened the door for him.

'Oh, Billy,' she said. 'Wha . . ?'

But she didn't have time to say any more, because Billy had rushed past her down the stairs. He tore through the kitchen, out through the back door and round the back of the house. There he missed his footing and tumbled across the lawn.

Something huge and clanky was moving on Mrs Batley's side of the fence. It was moving up the front path towards the place where Emma'd been standing. With a yelp Billy dived towards the fence. He squeezed and clawed his way under it and catapulted out on the other side.

The clanky thing was a lorry that had brought a load of bricks for Mrs Batley. Billy stood boldly in front of it and barked. At once a face peeped round the back of the lorry and glared at him.

'Hm! I see we've got another visitor,' said Mrs Batley, though not quite as sternly as usual.

'Billy!' cried Emma.

Billy was so pleased to hear her voice that he ran past the lorry onto Mrs Batley's lawn. Emma grabbed hold of his collar and pulled him back against the far hedge.

'Now hold him tight,' said Mrs Batley. 'Stay there and don't move. Don't get in the way.'

Sam the builder got out of the lorry's cab. He was going to build a patio at the back of Mrs Batley's house, so she could sit outside and watch the birds. He climbed up onto the back of the lorry and stood on top of the big cubes of bricks that were wrapped up in plastic and tied with ropes. Sam attached the rope on the first cube to a hook on a small crane. Then he stood back and, with a remote control, he made the crane lift up the bricks and swing them slowly sideways.

Mrs Batley stood close by watching carefully in case Sam ruined her flower border. Once the first cube of bricks had been safely lowered onto the path, Sam went on to the next.

All of a sudden Billy growled. Emma said 'Sh!' in a worried voice, but Billy couldn't stop himself.

Billy had heard a noise coming from the direction of the lorry. It was a noise so very sly and very thin that no one else had noticed it at all. Mrs Batley and Sam were talking as if nothing was wrong and Emma was concentrating hard on being quiet.

The noise got louder and louder in Billy's ears. It sounded like a monster quietly and sneakily bursting out of his chains.

Billy couldn't stand it any more. He leapt out of Emma's arms.

Emma squealed.

Mrs Batley gasped as Billy came charging at her and pushed her across the grass.

Sam the builder yelled.

Then all other noises were drowned as the rope holding the load of bricks snapped and the bricks fell roaring and crashing onto the ground.

'Billy!' cried Emma.

Billy turned tail and ran for his life. He jumped over the bricks, plunged under the fence, tore across the lawn, raced through the kitchen, dived into the deepest darkest corner under the stairs and pushed his nose tight against the wall.

Chapter 8

When Billy heard Emma's voice at the front door, he didn't move. Emma had someone else with her and he was scared of that someone.

'Mam! Dad!' shouted Emma.

'Ye-es,' sang Mam cheerily.

'Mam!' called Emma again.

Mam came out of the front room and she got scared too. Mrs Batley was on the doorstep.

'Oh!' said Mam in a panic. 'What's wrong? Has Billy been annoying you again? I'm sorry . . .' Mam gulped and stopped. She had just noticed the big smile on Emma's face.

Mrs Batley spoke in a loud, firm voice.

'If there is anything wrong, it's my fault,' she said. 'I've come round to apologise.'

'Apologise?' said Mam in amazement.

'Yes,' said Mrs Batley. 'I've been a very poor neighbour. Much too sharp and impatient. I feel very ashamed of myself, especially as Emma has been so kind to me.'

'Emma?' said Mam, looking more amazed still.

'She's been sending me such kind and friendly cards,' said Mrs Batley, taking Emma's latest picture from her jacket pocket. It was a picture of Billy with a happy robin standing on his head. 'Emma is a very fine girl, whom I'm proud to have living next door to me. And, of course, I'm very pleased to be living next door to Billy too.'

'Billy?' said Mam faintly.

'If it hadn't been for Billy I could well have had a very nasty accident,' said Mrs Batley, putting her arm round Emma's shoulder. 'Billy's a star.'

Tom and Catrin had been listening in their bedrooms. When they heard the words, "Billy's a star," they couldn't wait any longer. Their bedroom doors were flung open and they both came tumbling down the stairs. Dad appeared from the front room.

'What was that?' said Dad.

'Billy's a star,' said Emma excitedly. 'A load of bricks nearly fell on Mrs Batley, but Billy pushed her away.'

'It's true,' said Mrs Batley. 'He really did that. I was standing on the very spot where the bricks fell. One more second and I'd have been badly injured.'

'Billy growled,' said Emma.

'He must have heard the rope give way,' said Mrs Batley. 'His sense of hearing must be excellent.'

Billy forgot about hiding and sat up. Mrs Batley was right! His hearing really was brilliant! He gave a little yap of excitement.

'Billy!' said Emma, rushing to him.

'Billy!' said the rest of the Jones family, crowding around as Emma carried him out from under the stairs.

Billy was led into the front room, where everyone, including Mrs Batley, made a fuss of him. He sat beside her on Emma's lap which felt much more comfortable and friendly than a golden chair.

After that Mrs Batley went round the town telling everyone about her new friends, Billy and Emma.

That was how Billy became famous.

Soon photographers and journalists came ringing at the door of No. 7 Panteg Road.

Billy appeared on telly.

His photograph appeared in all the papers.

He even barked on the radio and featured on his very own website.

He had loads and loads of fanmail in which everyone said what an extra-clever dog he'd been. He was the hero who had saved Mrs Batley from a very nasty accident.

But that wasn't all that Billy had done.

He had made Emma sing again. From the day that he rescued Mrs Batley, Emma sang and sang. And whenever Emma sang, Billy stopped and listened. It didn't matter where he was – in the garden, in the front room or even next door in Mrs Batley's house – he always stopped and listened. After all, he was the listening member of the Jones family.

His ears had made him a star.

From the author . . .

One day, in a newspaper, I saw a photo of a small dog sitting on a chair in front of three judges. He was trying for a part in a musical show.

I pretended his name was Billy and this is his story.

I hope you like it.